Little Owl
in the Snow

Written by Christine Tagg ❋ Illustrated by Stephanie Boey

TEMPLAR

It was getting dark and Little Owl was all alone.
His mother had gone in search of supper. Little Owl gazed
across the snow from his cozy nest, high on a ledge.

"When the dark meets the light Mommy will return," he told
himself, and he waited… and waited… and waited.

Plump white snowflakes floated through the sky. If Little Owl listened he could hear them whispering.

shush, shush

Then he heard another sound.

crunch, crunch

"Mommy?" he called, but there was no reply. His large round eyes grew larger and rounder.

creak, creak

Little Owl turned his head as far as it would go, which was quite far, but still there was no sign of his mommy.

But wait, what could he see below in the snow?

Footprints! Fresh, frosty footprints. Mommy-sized footprints! Little Owl wriggled out of his nest and leaned over the edge, just a little too far... *flumph!*

Little Owl landed beak first in a snowdrift. He shook the cold from his feathers and started to follow the footprints. They led him to a creature with a shiny black nose.

"My Mommy doesn't have a shiny black nose," said Little Owl sadly, as the Fox shook his bushy tail, and disappeared into the dusk.

Little Owl saw more footprints. They lead him to a creature with long twitchy whiskers.

"My mommy doesn't have whiskers," said Little Owl, as the
Arctic Hare flicked out her legs and scampered away.

Little Owl trudged along the footprint path until he met four long legs. "My Mommy doesn't have long legs," he said, as the Reindeer shook her glistening antlers, and showered Little Owl with snowflakes.

"Nooo," she agreed. "But I dooo!"

On and on went Little Owl, following some really large
footprints now, until he came face to foot with the
biggest feet he had ever seen.

"My mommy doesn't have feet as big and furry as these,"
he said, as he looked up into the face of a great big Polar Bear!

Little Owl hurried on as fast as he could after that, until he saw something that made his heart leap for joy.

A feather! The whitest, softest, loveliest feather — *ever!*

"My mommy has feathers!" he cried excitedly, but the Snow Goose, to whom the feather belonged, simply said, "Honk," and flew away.

What was worse, Little Owl discovered that the footprint trail had lead him back to the very spot where he had fallen from his nest.

He began to cry and his tears made little prints of their own in the snow.

Little Owl was so upset that he did not hear his Mother land softly beside him.

"Where have you been?" she asked, and Little Owl told her all about the trail of footprints.

"But owls don't leave footprints!" Mother Owl laughed.

"Why not?" asked Little Owl.

"Because they fly, silly!"

And she beat her wings to show him. Little Owl beat his wings, too.

Flap, flap, flap, they went.